This Book Belongs to

Miss Anderson

©1992 CTP

The Long Blue Blazer

BY JEANNE WILLIS

ILLUSTRATED BY SUSAN VARLEY

E. P. DUTTON · NEW YORK

Text copyright © 1987 by Jeanne Willis
Illustrations copyright © 1987 by Susan Varley
First published in the United States 1988 by E. P. Dutton,
2 Park Avenue, New York, N.Y. 10016,
a division of NAL Penguin Inc.

Originally published in Great Britain 1987
by Andersen Press Ltd.,
62–65 Chandos Place, London WC2.

Printed by Grafiche AZ, Verona, Italy.

First American Edition   OBE   10 9 8 7 6 5 4 3 2 1

Library of Congress Cataloging-in-Publication Data
Willis, Jeanne.
   The long blue blazer.
   Summary: The new boy in class wears a long blue
blazer which he refuses to take off for any activity.
Only later does a classmate inadvertently discover his
secret.
   [1.Schools—Fiction.   2.Extraterrestrial beings—
Fiction]   I. Varley, Susan, ill.   II. Title.
PZ7.W68313Lo   1987   [E]   87-24453
ISBN 0-525-44381-9

Once there was a boy in my class who wore a long blue blazer. He had short arms and short legs and big feet that stuck out from under his long blue blazer.

He arrived one winter day. He wandered into the classroom, dusted with snow, and shook hands with the teacher.

She said, "You must be Wilson, the new boy."

The teacher told him to hang up his things. He took off his cap and his scarf and his mittens. But he wouldn't take off his long blue blazer.

The teacher asked him to, but he said he was cold. So she let him keep it on.

Later we did some painting. We all had to put plastic aprons on, but Wilson wore his apron over his long blue blazer.

I painted my mother wearing a pink flowery dress, and Mary painted her mother wearing green striped pants.

But Wilson painted his mother in a long blue blazer.

He ate his school lunch in his long blue blazer. He did his math in his long blue blazer. He went to gym class in his long blue blazer.

The teacher asked him to take it off, but he said his mother would be angry if he did. So she let him keep it on.

When it was time to go home, my mother came to get me. But nobody came for Wilson.

He stood alone in his long blue blazer, staring at the sky. The teacher asked him why his mother hadn't come to pick him up. He said she had a very long way to come.

Wilson walked slowly through the school gates, his long blue blazer dragging in the snow.

The teacher spoke to my mother. She told me to run after Wilson and invite him to come home with us.

That seemed to make him happy. But later when my mother asked him to take off his long blue blazer, he looked as if he was about to cry. So she let him keep it on.

She gave him some dinner and sat him on her lap. He put his arms around her and started to cry. He said he was tired.

Mom carried Wilson up to my bedroom
and sat him on a chair while she got him
some pajamas. When she came back, he'd
climbed into the top bunk in his long blue
blazer, and pulled the blankets around
him. I slept in the bottom bunk.

Later that night, a loud humming noise woke me up. I saw green and yellow flashing lights outside, and there, standing on the windowsill, was Wilson.

Suddenly...

he jumped!

The last I ever saw of him was his long
blue TAIL!